THE ANT BULLY

Story and pictures by JOHN NICKLE

SCHOLASTIC PRESS ■ NEW YORK

Copyright © 1999 by John Nickle
All rights reserved. Published by Scholastic Press,
a division of Scholastic Inc., PUBLISHERS SINCE 1920.
SCHOLASTIC and SCHOLASTIC PRESS and associated logos
are trademarks and/or registered trademarks of
Scholastic Inc.

Nickle, John
The ant bully / John Nickle. — 1st ed.
p.   cm.
Summary: Lucas learns a lesson about bullying when
he is pulled into the ant hole he
has been tormenting.
ISBN: 0-590-39591-2
(hardcover: alk. paper)
[1. Ants — Fiction.

2. Bullies —
Fiction.] I. Title
PZ7.N5584An 1998
[E] — dc21   98-19970
CIP   AC
10 9 8 7 6 5 4   02 03
Printed in Mexico   49

First edition, March 1999
The illustrations in this book were painted
in acrylics.
The text type was set in 15-point Base 9.
Book design by Kristina Iulo Albertson

But the ants had seen him first.

It was Sid the bully!

The wizard trickled potion drops into Lucas's ear until he slowly fell asleep. The ants laid him outside in the tall, soft grass. The next morning, Lucas awoke to an alarming sight.

Back at the ant colony, the Queen was very sad. Speedy and Rene had returned, but not Lucas. . . .

Then, to her delight, Lucas arrived! The Queen said, "Young man, you have been so brave, and you have learned the ways of the ants well. Your courage will be rewarded." She told the Ant Wizard to fill his dropper with growth potion.

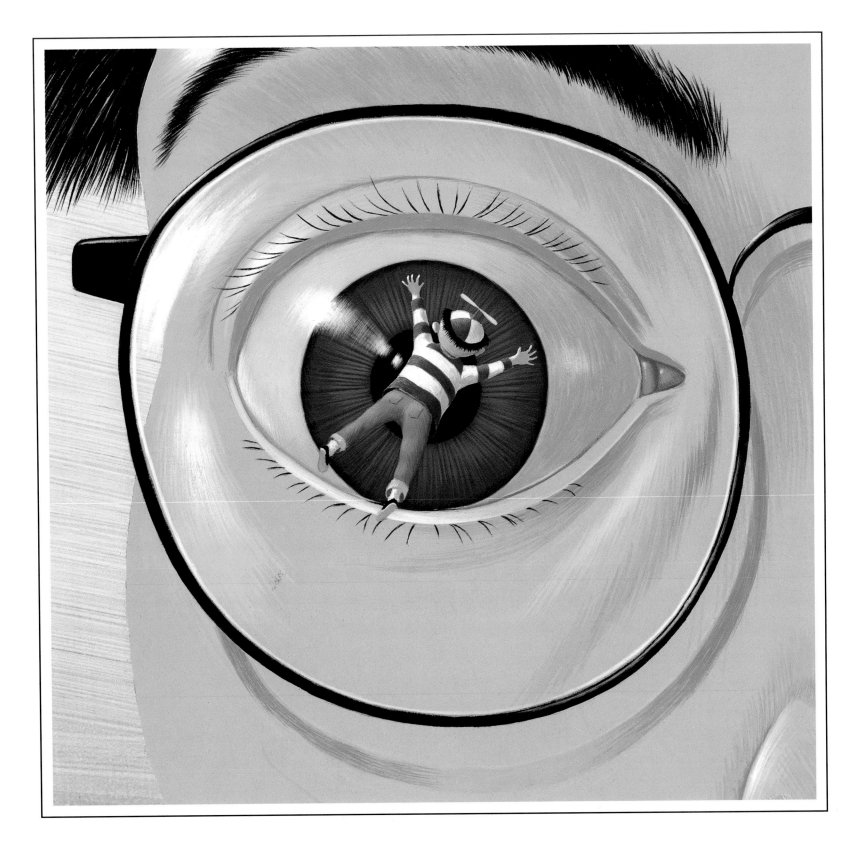

Lucas jumped at his father's face
so Speedy and Rene could escape!

"NO!" Lucas yelled.

His father stopped and looked closer.

But just as they were about to make off with their prize,
bright lights flashed and a booming voice filled the room.
"A N N N N T S !" Lucas's father bellowed.

When the last light was turned off, they quietly
snuck into the kitchen to find the Swell Jell.

"I was no giant," replied Lucas. "Not compared with Sid the bully.
He was always stealing my hat and spraying me with the hose."

"Oh, like you did to us?" said Speedy and Rene together.

After an awkward silence, the three set out for Lucas's house.

As they waited for the cover of night, the two ants had many questions for their new friend.

"What was it like to be a giant?" asked Speedy.

"Were you the biggest giant?" Rene wanted to know.

The Queen, however, was pleased and told Lucas that she would set him free if he passed one final test.

"You must go home and bring me a red Swell Jell."

"But I will need help," Lucas pleaded. "We ants always work together. How else could we gather food, defend ourselves, or please our queen?"

The Queen smiled and said, "Take Speedy and Rene with you. They are upstairs."

But the worst part of his sentence was
attending the Queen with the drones.

and spiders.

Defending the colony against wasps . . .

gathering food too.

hard labor with the worker ants . . .

"G U I L T Y !"
thundered the judge.
Lucas's sentence was harsh . . .

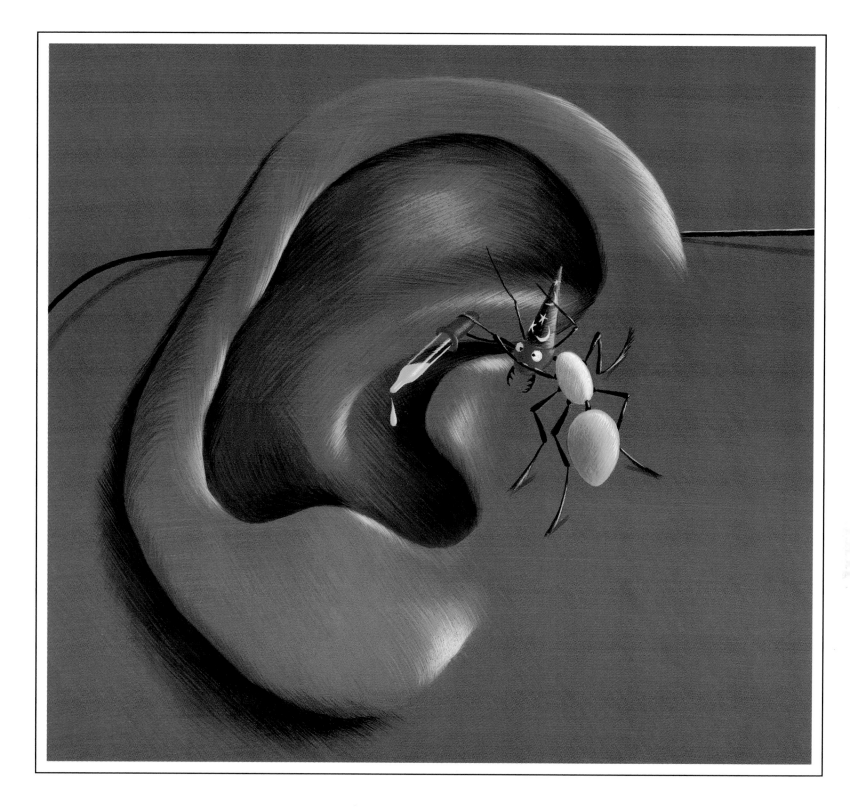

Lucas was too stunned to respond. The Queen took his silence as a further insult. She turned to the Ant Wizard and said, "Shrink this boy! And put him on trial!"

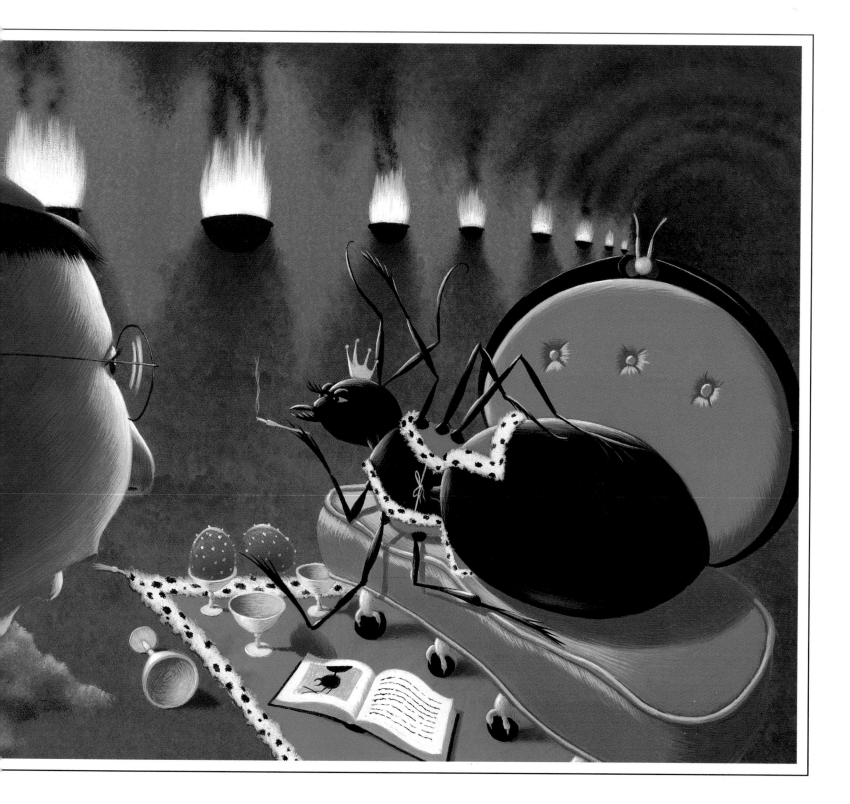

Coolly, she looked him over. "So you are the one who
always floods my colony. Don't you realize how long and
hard we work to build what you destroy in seconds?"

With great skill and team effort, they stuffed Lucas's large body into their ant hole and forced him into the Queen's chamber.

and soon they had had enough.

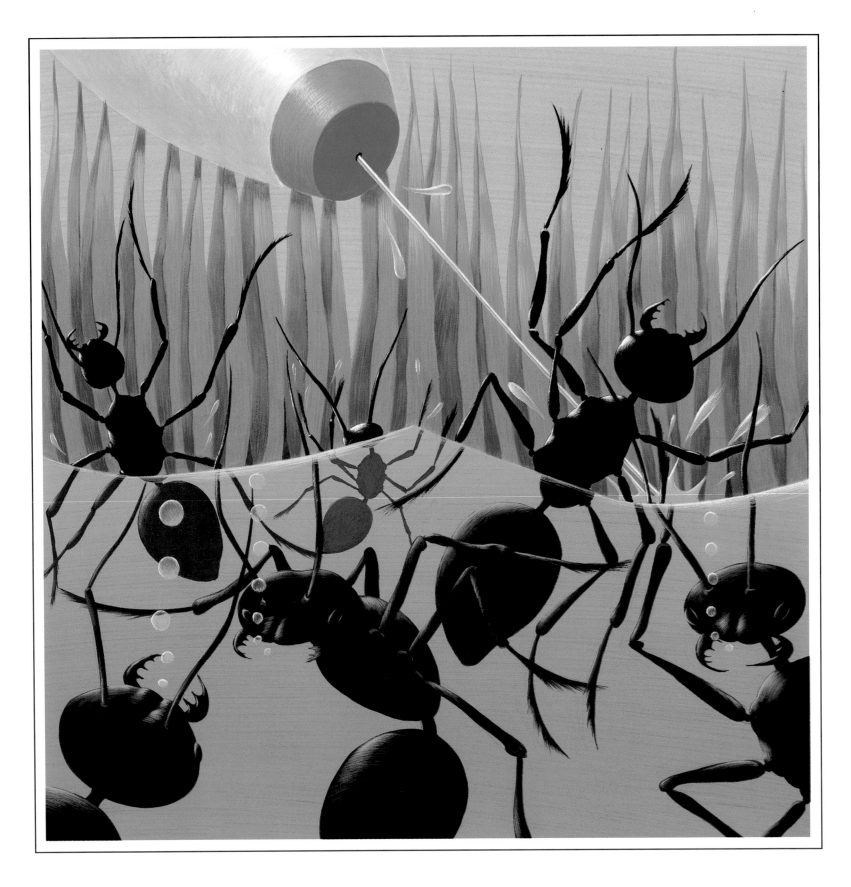

But the ants didn't like to get wet . . .

So Lucas bullied the ants.

Lucas wore funny glasses and a strange hat. Some kids thought he was weird. Sid the neighborhood bully was especially mean to him.

TO *Mom and Dad*

FOR GIVING ME THAT FIRST CRAYON

AND TO *Jana*

FOR NOT TAKING IT AWAY.

VERY SPECIAL THANKS TO *Tracy Mack*

FOR MAKING MY STORY BETTER.

Nickle, John
The ant bully / John Nickle. — 1st ed.
p.   cm.
Summary: Lucas learns a lesson about bullying when
he is pulled into the ant hole he
has been tormenting.
ISBN: 0-590-39591-2
(hardcover: alk. paper)
[1. Ants — Fiction.

2. Bullies —
Fiction.] I. Title
PZ7.N5584An 1998
[E] — dc21   98-19970
CIP   AC
10 9 8 7 6 5 4   02 03
Printed in Mexico   49

First edition, March 1999
The illustrations in this book were painted
in acrylics.
The text type was set in 15-point Base 9.
Book design by Kristina Iulo Albertson